Max and Molly's
Guide To Trouble

How To Catch A Criminal

DOMINIC BARKER

ILLUSTRATED BY HANNAH SHAW

ORCHARD BOOKS

ORCHARD BOOKS
338 Euston Road, London NW1 3BH
Orchard Books Australia
Hachette Children's Books
Level 17/207 Kent Street, Sydney, NSW 2000

First published in 2011 by Orchard Books

ISBN 978 1 40830 519 5

Orchard Books is a division of Hachette Children's Books,
an Hachette UK company.

www.hachette.co.uk

SNAP, CRACKLE AND CRUNCH

"Mix everything together, Molly," urged Max.

It was breakfast time at 42 Laburnum Avenue and twins Max and Molly Pesker were developing a recipe for the best breakfast cereal in the world.

They had been at it now for about half an hour and they were almost there...

Mum came into the kitchen.

"Look at all this mess!" she said.

Max and Molly surveyed the mess briefly. Open jars and packets covered every surface.

"You have to make a mess when you're inventing something new," explained Molly. "It shows you've been doing it right."

"Did you know," Max asked his mum, "that Alexander Fleming only discovered penicillin because he was messy? If he'd been tidy we might all be *very ill*."

"I'll be *very ill* if the kitchen isn't tidied up straightaway," said Mum. "I'm going to have a shower and I expect it to be spotless when I come back."

Mum disappeared upstairs.

"She wants the mess to be gone when she comes back from her shower," said Max.

"But she didn't tell us how long her shower was going to be," said Molly.

"Did she look dirty to you?" asked Max.

"Not on the bits of her I could see," admitted Molly. "But she had her dressing gown on. She could have been very dirty under that."

"Which means she'll have to have a really long shower," said Max.

So Max and Molly put off the tidying up and put the finishing touches to their new breakfast cereal instead.

"It needs a name," said Molly when they were done. "One that's different from every other cereal so people will remember it."

"How about

BLACK WIDOW CRUNCHIES?"

suggested Max.

"Isn't the Black Widow a **POISONOUS SPIDER**?" said Molly doubtfully.

Max nodded. "People like poisonous things," he explained. "They're always making programmes about them on TV."

Whenever Max wanted to reassure someone he always told them a horrible fact about the natural world. It didn't always work.

"OK," said Molly. "Now we've got a name, all we need is someone to eat it."

"I'll eat it," said Max.

Molly shook her head. "You already know how nice it is," she said. "If we're going to do it properly then we're going to have to try it on someone who has no idea."

"Who do we know who has no idea?" said Max.

They thought for a moment.

"Dad!"

TASTE TEST

Max and Molly's dad was sitting in the garden, enjoying the morning sun and reading the **The Trull Gazette**.

"Dad," said Molly, with a full bowl of **BLACK WIDOW CRUNCHIES** in her hands.

"There've been three more robberies,"
said Dad, not looking up from the paper.
"One of them was in Park Road."

Park Road was next to their road,
Laburnum Avenue.

"We've brought you some breakfast,"
said Molly, popping the bowl down
beside Dad.

"Mrs Lynch lost all her jewellery,"
continued Dad. "The thief pretends to
be from an insurance company. He gains
old people's trust by telling them they're
owed some money, and that he can hand
it over if they show him proof of their
identity. While the victim is looking
for it, he sneaks around the house,
pocketing their valuables."

   Without letting his eyes leave the
paper he helped himself to a large
spoonful of breakfast.

Dad went very pale. "What was that?" he gasped.

"It's our new cereal," explained Molly. **"BLACK WIDOW CRUNCHIES!"** said Max.

"It's horrible," spluttered Dad.

"It can't be," insisted Molly. "We put everything people like for breakfast into a bowl and mixed it together."

"What do you mean, everything people like?" said Dad.

"There's **cornflakes**

and toast and jam

and **marmalade**

and **grapefruit**

and eggs," said Max.

"And **peanut butter**

and orange juice

and sugar

and **pickle**,"

added Molly enthusiastically.

"**Pickle?**" shuddered Dad. "People don't have **pickle** for breakfast!"

"I picked up the wrong jar," explained Molly. "But we'd put in so many things already that it seemed a shame to start again."

"Do you think it needs more milk?" asked Max.

"It needs throwing away," said Dad. "IT'S DISGUSTING!"

"Did you know that a vampire bat can drink half its weight in blood in less than twenty minutes?" asked Max.

But Dad just stomped off to get
a drink and wash away the taste of
BLACK WIDOW CRUNCHIES.

"I think it probably needs another
ingredient," Max reflected.

Molly thought
for a second.
"Ice cream?"

BUMP IT UP!

After they had tidied the kitchen,
Max and Molly went into the garden
to play **Forugbasnet. Forugbasnet**
was a combination of football, rugby,
basketball and netball. Max and Molly
were the only people in the whole world

who knew the rules of **Forugbasnet**,
because they had invented them.

Max played a particularly skilful shot
which involved bouncing the ball off
the guinea pig's cage, against the garage
and over the top branch of the big tree
at the bottom of the garden.

"Wow!" exclaimed Molly.

The ball disappeared over the fence
they shared with Mrs Quibble.

A few seconds later they heard a
muffled cry.

"Ow!"

Max and Molly rushed to the fence
and scrambled up it as fast as they
could. One of the rules of **Forugbasnet**
was that you got an extra point if you
got the ball back first.

Their two heads popped over the
top of the fence at exactly the same
moment.

"Can we have our ball back, please,
Mrs Quibble?" they yelled.

Mrs Quibble was an old lady. She had a reputation for being kind, friendly and particularly fond of children. This reputation had been sorely tested by Max and Molly.

"Do you know how many times this ball has come into my garden in the last week?" she asked.

"No," said Max truthfully.

"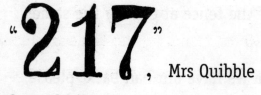" , Mrs Quibble informed him.

"We have been playing **Forugbasnet**
a lot," agreed Max.

"But," continued Mrs Quibble,
"this is the first time that it has
landed on my head."

"Do you think you should get an
extra point for that?" Molly asked Max.

"I beg your pardon?" said
Mrs Quibble.

"Please can we have our ball back?"
said Molly, changing the subject quickly.

Mrs Quibble stared hard at the twins.
Max and Molly responded with their

sweetest smiles. But Mrs Quibble wasn't
to be won over. She could already feel a
bump growing on her head.

"No," she said. "You can't."

"But we're halfway through a game,"
said Max.

"And we did say please," Molly
pointed out.

"I don't care," said Mrs Quibble.

"Two hundred and seventeen times
is enough. This ball is going into
my house and it's staying there.
For good."

"But..." said Max and Molly.

"I've heard quite enough," said
Mrs Quibble. "And to make sure
I don't hear any more I'm
turning my hearing aid off."

And she did exactly that. Then she
stalked up the path to her back door
with their ball gripped tightly in
her hands.

CRIME BUT NO PUNISHMENT

PC Truncheon was having a stressful day. His boss, Inspector Formfill, had read the headlines in **The Trull Gazette**. He had made it very clear that he wanted the **criminal** responsible for all the local robberies arrested very soon, because

it was making a mess of
his statistics. And there was
nothing Inspector Formfill liked
less than messy statistics.

Still, however stressful PC Truncheon's
day had been so far, it was about to
get worse.

He looked up to see two children
with red hair standing in front of the
reception desk. The boy was wearing
a green T-shirt and combat trousers.
The girl was wearing a white dress
with multicoloured spots on it.

"Evening 'all,"
said PC Truncheon.

"It's morning," corrected Max.
"I'm Max and this is Molly. We've come
to report a **crime**."

"A very **serious crime**," stressed Molly.

"Really?" said PC Truncheon
doubtfully. Apart from the recent
burglaries Trull had very little **serious
crime**.

"We've been robbed," said Max.

"While playing in our own garden,"
added Molly.

PC Truncheon studied the
children's faces.

They certainly looked sincere.

Could it be that they too had become victims of the local burgler? PC Truncheon had been secretly hoping he would strike again in case he left a clue which might lead to his capture. He decided to give the matter his full attention. He picked up his special **Serious Crimes Pen**.

"Start at the beginning and give me all the details," he said. "An experienced policeman like myself is trained to spot clues that civilians like yourselves would overlook, so leave nothing out."

Max was happy to oblige. "I was born in Trull Hospital eight years ago," he began, "and then twelve minutes later Molly was born. So we're twins but I'm older—"

"He's always going on about it," interrupted Molly. "You'd think something special happened in those twelve minutes."

"It did," insisted Max. "I did lots of growing. That's why I'm taller."

"Only one centimetre," said Molly grumpily.

"Anyway," continued Max. "Like I was saying, twenty minutes later Molly was born and—"

PC Truncheon held up his special **Serious Crimes Pen** for silence.

"I'm starting at the beginning and I'm leaving nothing out," said Max.

"I meant, leave nothing out about the robbery," said PC Truncheon.

"You didn't say that," pointed out Molly, who felt she should stick up for her brother.

"I'm making it clear now," said PC Truncheon, a trifle testily.

"Right," said Max. "We were playing in the garden and the ball hit the guinea pig's cage."

PC Truncheon raised his special **Serious Crimes Pen** once more. "Is the guinea pig's cage strictly relevant?" he demanded.

"Of course it is," said Molly. "We were playing **Forugbasnet**. The guinea pig's cage is the most important thing. Don't you know anything?"

PC Truncheon gripped his special **Serious Crimes Pen** tightly and said nothing.

Max continued with his explanation of the robbery. He made sure that he left nothing out...

...Mrs Quibble...

...the **217** times that
the ball had gone into her garden...the
bump on her head...her refusal to return
the ball...and finally her promise to
keep it *for ever*.

"But because she's old we don't want
her to go to jail," finished Max.

"Well, maybe for a few days, Max,"
said Molly. "Just to make sure she's
learnt her lesson."

They looked at PC Truncheon
expectantly.

PC Truncheon put down his special **Serious Crimes Pen**. He stared very hard at the twins.

"Is there something wrong with your eyes?" asked Molly, noticing that they were beginning to bulge.

"There is nothing wrong with my eyes," said PC Truncheon. "What is wrong is that you two hooligans can throw your ball—"

"Kick," corrected Max.

PC Truncheon's eyes bulged a little

more. "*Kick* your ball into the garden of an elderly lady, on multiple occasions, finally resulting in a head injury. And when said old lady refuses to return your ball, you report her to the police. I don't know *what* the world is coming to!"

Molly had been distracted by the purple colour that PC Truncheon was turning and had forgotten to listen to what he was saying.

"Are you going to arrest her and get our ball back?" she asked.

PC Truncheon's eyes bulged out so far that there seemed a good chance they might pop out of his head and jump across the desk.

I AM NOT GOING TO ARREST HER!

he bellowed.

I'VE A GOOD MIND TO ARREST YOU!

"Would you arrest her if I promised to tell you the name of the most **venomous snake** in Australia?" asked Max.

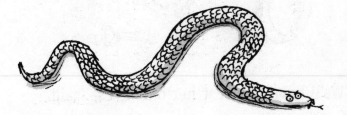

It turned out that PC Truncheon wouldn't.

CRIME PREVENTION

"We'll have to arrest her ourselves," said Max when they were back outside the police station.

"Can we do that?" asked Molly.

Max nodded. "We can perform a **CITIZEN'S ARREST.**"

"What's that?" asked Molly.

Max explained that anybody could arrest someone if there was a **crime** being committed and there were no police there to do the arresting for them.

"Wow!" said Molly. "If I'd known that before I'd have arrested lots of people."

"Like who?"

"Like Miss Bailey. And Toby Surplice."

"What did Miss Bailey do?"

"She set us way too much homework and it was too hard."

"It's got to be for a *real* **crime**," explained Max. "And I don't think setting too much homework is a *real* **crime**."

"Toby Surplice then," said Molly. "He burped in my ear. That must be a **crime**. It was disgusting."

Max shook his head. He was pretty sure burping in someone's ear wasn't a **crime**.

"It should be," said Molly. "I'm going to write to the government about it. Who's the **Minister for Burps?**"

"We'll find out later," Max assured her. "But stealing is definitely a **crime** so we should arrest Mrs Quibble now."

Suddenly Molly felt doubtful. "Mrs Quibble is usually quite nice," she said. "Maybe we should let her off. For good behaviour."

"No, Molly," said Max firmly. "Don't you remember what Mr Leavold said in assembly last week?"

Mr Leavold was the Head Teacher at Trull School.

"No," said Molly. "I was trying to see
if he wears a wig and it was taking
up all my concentration."

"He said that you shouldn't be even a little bit naughty because once you've been a little bit naughty then next time you do something it's a bit **more** naughty and the time after that it's even **more** naughty and before you know it you're a **murderer**."

"A **murderer!**" said Molly, her eyes wide.

Max nodded.

"Do you think Mrs Quibble is going to be a **murderer** now?" asked Molly.

"Not if we stop her in time," explained Max. "If we arrest her she'll see that stealing our ball was bad and then she'll realise the error of her ways and go back to being a kind old lady."

"So we're actually helping her?" said Molly.

Max nodded.

"In that case," said Molly, "the sooner we arrest her, the better."

They set off running towards
Mrs Quibble's house.

Suddenly Max stopped,
a worried frown on his face.

"What's the matter?"
said Molly.

"We can't just arrest her,"
he said. "Before we do
we've got to get her to
admit that she stole the
ball from us. That's called
a **CONFESSION**. Otherwise the police
might let her go."

"I don't think she'll confess," said Molly. "Even if we say please twice."

"You're right," agreed Max. "She'll be on her guard. We'll have to get somebody she wouldn't suspect to make her admit what she's done, and then we can pounce."

Max and Molly looked at each other and said the same word at the same time.

"Peter!"

PETERING IN

"Achoo!" said Peter.

"Did you say yes?"
asked Molly.

"No," said Peter. "No!
No! N...Achoo!"

Peter was seven.
He lived on the same
street as Max and Molly.
He had brown hair that
stood up at the front and
he always had a cold.

"Don't make up your mind straight away," said Max.

But Peter didn't seem to have any problem making up his mind. He shook his head so violently that Molly thought it might fall off.

"We haven't told you what it's all about yet," she said sweetly.

"I don't care," said Peter. "My mum

said I must **never ever** play with you
two again because you always get me
into trouble."

"We don't want you to play with us.
It's much more important than that."

"It's extra ultra important," added Max.

Despite his mother's orders, Peter
couldn't help himself. "What is it?"
he asked.

"It's not worth telling you now," said
Molly, looking sad. "Because you've
already said you won't help us. That's
right, isn't it, Max?"

Max nodded.

"And we were saying all the way here that Peter was the only one who could help us solve this **crime**," added Molly.

"**Crime?**" said Peter. That sounded interesting.

"Sssh, Max," said Molly. "Peter doesn't want to be involved."

"What **crime?** Come on! You've got to tell me."

Molly looked up and down the street to make sure there was nobody about who could overhear.

Peter could barely contain his excitement.

Molly beckoned him to come closer. *"Mrs Quibble has stolen our football,"* she revealed.

"Mrs Quibble!" repeated Peter. "But she's old. She doesn't play football."

"Are you on her side?" demanded Molly fiercely.

"No," protested Peter quickly. "It's just that what with her being an old age pensioner I didn't think she'd—"

"You *are* on her side," accused Molly. "You're making excuses because you want her to get away with it."

"I don't," said Peter. "It's just—"

Molly held up her hand to silence him.

"Come along, Max," she said. "We'll go and see if we can find someone else who'll help. Peter would obviously believe a thief before us, his oldest friends."

And turning on their heels, Max and Molly set off down Laburnum Avenue.

"Stop!" said Peter.

Max and Molly kept walking.

"I'll help!" said Peter.

This time Max and Molly stopped and turned round.

"What about your mum?" asked Molly.

"She wouldn't mind if it was a **crime**," said Peter, a little doubtfully. "She was reading **The Trull Gazette** this morning and going on about all the robberies, and she banged the table and said that somebody should do something about **crime**. Well I'm *somebody* and I'm going to do *something*."

And without knowing what that something was, Peter followed Max and Molly out of Laburnum Avenue.

JUST ANSWER
THE QUESTIONS

Mrs Quibble was in the kitchen listening
to Radio 4 when the doorbell rang.
When she opened the door she found
herself facing a boy. He had a tuft of
hair standing up at the front, and
he was wearing jeans and a T-shirt
with a Tyrannosaurus Rex on it.

"Hello," said Mrs Quibble.

"Achoo!" said the boy.

"Bless you," said Mrs Quibble. "What can I help you with?"

"I've forgotten," said the boy.

"Well, dear," said Mrs Quibble kindly. "I can't really help you if you've forgotten what it is you'd like help with."

"Wait a minute, please," said the boy. "Somebody wrote it down in case I forgot. I forget things when I'm nervous."

"There's no need to be nervous,"
Mrs Quibble assured him.

"Achoo!" sneezed the boy.
He fumbled in his pocket and pulled
out a piece of paper.

"I'm conducting a survey," he read, "as part of my school's study of the local neighbourhood. Would you help me by answering a few simple questions?"

"Of course, dear," said Mrs Quibble. "Ask away!"

"You'll probably want to see my identification first," said the boy. "Here it is."

The boy fished in his pocket and pulled out a crumpled piece of paper which he handed to Mrs Quibble. On it, in rather untidy handwriting, was written:

My name
is Peter.

"Hello, Peter," said Mrs Quibble.

"Hello, Mrs Quibble. Question one.
What is your name?"

"My name?" said Mrs Quibble, looking
puzzled. "You just said my name."

"Did I?" said Peter.

Mrs Quibble nodded.

"I knew this was too hard," muttered Peter.

"Keep trying," said Mrs Quibble kindly. "These school assignments can be difficult."

"What school... Oh yes," remembered Peter.

Mrs Quibble nodded encouragingly.

"Question two. Where do you live?"

"14 Park Road."

"Question three. Are you a **criminal**

who recently stole Max and Molly Pesker's football?"

Mrs Quibble didn't say anything.

"Shall I ask you again?" said Peter.

"That won't be necessary," said Mrs Quibble. "Could I ask *you* a question, Peter?"

"Er..." Peter looked unsure. "Nobody said anything about you asking questions."

"Do you—" began Mrs Quibble.

"Can I see your identification, please?" interrupted Peter.

"I don't need identification,
Peter. This is my house."

"Oh," said Peter.

"Do you know Max and Molly
Pesker, Peter?"

"Achoo!"

"Do you?"

"Er...might do."

"Did they tell you to come round here and ask me about this?"

"Er...can't remember."

"Could you tell them that the lump on my head is still growing and that they are not getting their ball back?"

"I'll tell them."

"So you do know them?"

"Yes... No... I don't know."

Peter was finding answering questions far more difficult than asking them.

"I think that's good enough for me," said Mrs Quibble. "Now if you'll excuse me, dear, it's time for *The Archers*."

Mrs Quibble closed her front door firmly.

"Achoo!" sneezed Peter.

TRAINERLESS TRAINING

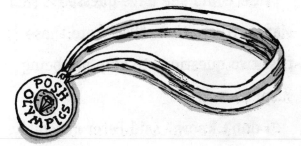

"You must have done something wrong," said Molly.

They had all retreated to the playground and were sitting on the roundabout.

"I didn't," protested Peter. "She just

suddenly guessed that you'd sent me when I asked her the third question."

"How could she have guessed?" said Max in frustration. "We wrote those first two questions to stop her being suspicious."

"I don't know," said Peter miserably. "Anyway, she said to tell you that the lump on her head was getting bigger and you weren't going to get your ball back."

Max suddenly stopped looking miserable. "Say that again," he said.

"Anyway, she said to tell you that the lump on her head was getting bigger and you weren't going to get your ball back," said Peter, again.

"Wow!" said Max.

"What is it?" asked Molly.

"Don't you see?" said Max. "She's made a **CONFESSION**. She said we can't have our football back. That means that she's got it and she's told you that she has, Peter."

"Did she?" said Peter.

"Yes." Max nodded vigorously. "That means that we can make a **CITIZEN'S ARREST**. Then when PC Truncheon comes you can tell him that Mrs Quibble admitted to you that she'd stolen our football. You're a *witness*."

"I don't like talking to PC Truncheon," said Peter nervously. "I did it once before and it made me sneeze really badly."

"But you have to," insisted Max. "If we don't arrest her quickly she might sell our ball on eBay to get rid of the evidence. We've got to do it now and then you can tell the police and they can search her house and we'll have solved a big **crime**."

"And if you don't she'll probably become a **murderer**," added Molly.

Peter opened his mouth to ask why.

But he didn't get the chance because
at that moment they were distracted by
a man in a suit and tie sprinting out of
Park Road towards them. As he ran into
the playground he tripped over the edge
of the seesaw and crashed onto
the grass.

"Are you all right?" called Molly.

They jumped off the roundabout and ran over to the man.

"Fine," said the man, getting rapidly to his feet. "I'm fine. Nothing to worry about. I was just out jogging."

"You should wear a tracksuit," suggested Molly. "It's better for running in."

"Thanks," said the man, rubbing the side of his head and looking about nervously. "Good idea."

"Did you know that the yellow fat-tailed scorpion kills more humans than any other scorpion?" asked Max, to take the man's mind off his injuries.

"No," admitted the man. "I didn't.

"And why aren't you wearing trainers?" persisted Molly. "That's weird."

"No, it's not," protested the man.

"It is," insisted Molly.

The man looked around nervously again. "Can you keep a secret?"

"Not normally," admitted Molly.

"Well, you should keep this one," said the man. "I'm training for the **Posh Olympics.**"

"What are they?"

"They're just like the normal Olympics," explained the man, "but in smart clothes. I've got a good chance of a medal."

"It looks like you've got enough jewellery already," observed Molly, looking behind him. "It fell out of your pockets when you fell over."

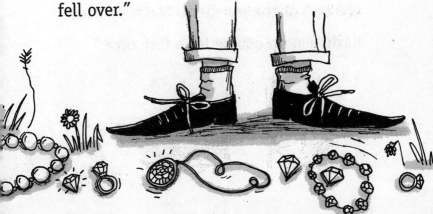

The man was startled. He spun round and looked at the bracelets and necklaces and rings that had tumbled out of his pockets.

"So I have," said the man, quickly picking them up. "In the **Posh Olympics** you have to carry valuable objects with you during events."

"Why?" asked Max.

"To show you're rich enough to enter," said the man, breathlessly scooping up the last of the jewellery. "Anyway. Must dash. I'm on course for a fast time."

"You've torn your trousers," said Molly.

But the man didn't appear to hear.

He dashed off across the playground,

heading for the road.

Max, Molly and Peter watched him go. Then they returned to the question of arresting Mrs Quibble and getting their ball back.

"The problem is this," continued Max. "If we just knock on Mrs Quibble's door and tell her she's arrested, she might try and escape."

"We could handcuff her to something," suggested Molly.

Max pointed out that handcuffing old ladies might get them into trouble. And anyway, they hadn't got any handcuffs.

"Hmm," said Molly.

"We need to find somewhere in her house to lock her up for a few minutes. Then we can ring the police and they can take her away and we can get our ball back."

"But she won't let us in her house," said Molly.

"I know," agreed Max. "We've got to find a way to get into her house without her knowing."

They pondered this for a while.

"What if," said Molly suddenly, "we gave her some news that surprised her so much that she rushed off without shutting her front door? Then we could sneak in and find a room to lock her up in."

"What news would make her do that?" wondered Peter.

"She likes gardening," said Max. "That's why she knows how many times our football has gone into her back garden in the last week, because she's always out there talking to her plants."

"What would make a gardener so surprised that they'd rush off and leave their front door open?" asked Molly.

The three of them sat in silence, thinking.

"**Moles**," said Peter suddenly. "My mum likes gardening and she hates **moles**."

"**Moles** could work," agreed Max. "All we need is for you to tell her that there's a hundred **moles** making a hundred **molehills** in the middle of her lawn. She'll drop everything and

rush into the back garden to stop
them and while she's distracted we'll
sneak in."

"But I can't tell her," protested Peter.
"She knows I'm your friend now."

This was definitely a problem.

But Molly had a solution. "Not if
you're in disguise."

PARDNERS IN CRIME

"I'm really not sure about this," said Peter.

"You've got to do it," said Molly. "Mrs Quibble could be a **murderer** by teatime."

Peter was standing in Max's bedroom wearing Max's cowboy outfit.

He had already refused to wear Molly's ballerina costume.

"I still think she might recognise me," said Peter.

"I know," said Molly, picking up a brown marker pen from her art box. "I'll give you a moustache. Then she'll never guess."

Quickly, she drew a thick brown moustache below Peter's nose.

"What does **INDELIBLE** mean?" asked Peter, studying the side of the pen.

"This is no time for learning big words, Peter," said Max. "We've got a **criminal** to catch."

"Are you sure that when I tell her there are **moles** in her back garden she'll just rush off and leave the door open?" asked Peter doubtfully.

"If you tell her properly," said Molly.

"You've got to sound really worried," said Max.

"I *am* really worried," said Peter.

"Then you'll be fine," said Molly.
"You've also got to sound like a cowboy so that she doesn't see through your disguise."

"How do they sound?" asked Peter.

"You say something like, **Howdy, Mrs Quibble, pardner. There's a wagonload of moles in your back garden and those pesky critters are making hills the size of rattlesnakes.**"

"Which species of rattlesnake?" asked Max.

"It doesn't matter," said Molly.

"I'm not sure that I can say that,"
said Peter.

"You've got to," said Max. "Or the plan
won't work."

"Couldn't I go home instead?"

"No," Molly told him firmly. "We're all
together in the fight against **crime**."

Five minutes later, Max, Molly and
Peter were crouched behind a bush by
the entrance to Mrs Quibble's front drive.

"Howdy, Mrs Quibble, pardner," Peter muttered to himself. **"Howdy, Mrs Quibble, pardner."**

"Go on," urged Max. "As soon as you've distracted her we'll sneak into the house."

"Achoo!" said Peter.

"If you *have* to sneeze," said Molly severely, "say **Achoo, pardner!**"

"Sorry," said Peter.

"Hurry up!" said Max.

Sighing, Peter stood and started up the drive.

"He's not walking right," said Max, watching critically from behind. "Cowboys walk with their legs further apart to stop their spurs catching on their ankles."

"Do you think she'll wonder where his horse is?" asked Molly suddenly.

"We'll have to hope that the news about the **moles** distracts her," said Max.

Peter got closer and closer to the door. Max and Molly held their breath...

Peter raised his hand to knock. And then stopped and pushed.

The door swung open on its own.

GENTLY
DOES IT

Max and Molly rushed to join Peter at
the door.

"It's already open!" exclaimed Peter.

"Whisper!" cautioned Molly.

"This is brilliant," hissed Max. "We can
find somewhere to lock Mrs Quibble up
without her even knowing we're here."

"But why do you think
the door is open?"
whispered Peter.

"We can't think about that now," said Max impatiently. "Me and Molly will check round the house. You go through to the garden and make sure Mrs Quibble isn't going to come in and catch us."

The three children crept stealthily into the house. There was no sign of Mrs Quibble.

Max pushed Peter towards the kitchen door which led to the garden. Then Max and Molly tiptoed along the hallway.

Suddenly they heard a *clunk*.

And then a *thump*.

It seemed to be coming from
the cupboard under the hall
stairs. They could see the door
was ajar and a light was on.
There was a rustle as though
somebody was searching
for something. It could
only be one person.

Mrs Quibble.

Max and Molly looked at each other,
their eyes gleaming with excitement.

And then Max spotted something.
The door had a key! It would take just
a second to slip across, close the door
and lock it.

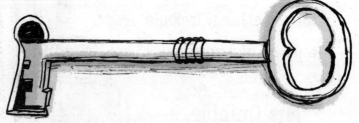

The twins flew silently across the hall.
Max shut the door and Molly turned the
key. Mrs Quibble was caught!

Not only was she caught, she was **angry.** She shook the door handle vigorously and hammered on the door.

"We are conducting a **CITIZEN'S ARREST**," Max informed the door. "We will alert the police."

"It's for your own good," explained Molly.

The door knob was shaken even harder.

"Let's find the phone, Molly," said Max, "and call PC Truncheon."

They rushed to look for the phone. They found it in the lounge. Next to it was a football. *Their* football.

Proof! Mrs Quibble was caught red-handed. Shaking with excitement, Max picked up the phone and dialled.

"Trull Police Station. PC Truncheon speaking."

"Hello. This is Max Pesker. I'm ringing to report a **CITIZEN'S ARREST**."

"A what... Who?"

"Max Pesker."

"Is this some kind of joke, lad?"

"No. We've have the **criminal** in custody at 14 Park Road."

PC Truncheon was puzzled. "What do you mean *in custody*?"

"Locked in a cupboard."

PC Truncheon was confused.

"Are you one of those kids with red hair who was here this morning?"

"Yes."

"Don't tell me..." PC Truncheon sounded incredulous. "Don't tell me you've locked that poor old lady in a cupboard. *I don't believe it!* Inspector Formfill will go crazy. Stay where you are. I'll be there in two minutes."

The phone went dead.

"He's coming," said Max, putting down the handset. "I think he's very impressed. He said he couldn't believe it."

"He'll be even more impressed when he sees we've got the evidence," said Molly, as she went to pick up the ball.

"Don't touch it!" shouted Max. "He'll probably want to dust it for fingerprints."

A loud banging on the door of the cupboard drew them back into the hall.

"I don't think Mrs Quibble understands that we're saving her from being a **murderer**," said Molly.

The door banged even harder.

What on earth is going on?

Max and Molly looked up in surprise.
Standing at the top of the stairs was
Mrs Quibble.

"Max and Molly Pesker?" she said. "What are you doing in my house?"

"What are you doing not in the cupboard?" demanded Molly.

Mrs Quibble was perplexed. "What do you mean, what am I doing not in the cupboard? Why should I be in the cupboard? I went upstairs to get my birth certificate for Mr Clements so I can claim the insurance money he owes me. It was right at the back of the—"

Before she could finish the front door
burst open and PC Truncheon charged
into the hall.

"It's all right, Mrs Quibble!" he shouted. "I'll get you out!"

"I beg your pardon, Constable," said Mrs Quibble from the top of the stairs.

PC Truncheon looked up. "Oh," he said. "You've escaped."

"What an extraordinary thing to say," said Mrs Quibble. "What do you mean, I've escaped?"

PC Truncheon looked at Max and Molly. And then back at Mrs Quibble.

"I was under the impression that these two had locked you up."

"Locked me up, Constable?" said Mrs Quibble. "Why on earth would they do that?"

"I believe these children will be able to shed some light on these matters," he muttered, advancing threateningly across the hall towards Max and Molly.

Intrigued, Mrs Quibble made her way downstairs as fast as she could...

Max and Molly gulped.

Just then there
was a bang from
inside the hall
cupboard.

"What's that?" said PC Truncheon.

"What's going on in my
cupboard?" said Mrs Quibble.

"Er..." said Max.

"Double er..." said Molly.

"And where's Mr Clements?" she
demanded, looking stonily at Max
and Molly.

"You two are going to have an awful lot of explaining to do," said PC Truncheon grimly.

He pushed past the twins and unlocked the door. To Max and Molly's astonishment, out of the cupboard came the man who'd been training for the Posh Olympics. They had locked up a potential medal-winner!

"We can explain,"
said Max desperately.
"Can we?" asked Molly.
"Mr Clements,"
said Mrs Quibble
in horror. "I'm so sorry. I just—"
"Mr Clements indeed," interrupted
PC Truncheon. "His real name is Harry
the Gent – a notorious local **criminal**.
We've had our eye on him for the recent
robberies but we've never been able to
catch him in the act."

But that is precisely what Max and Molly had done. **Harry the Gent's** pockets bulged with jewellery.

"That's my gold bracelet," said
Mrs Quibble.

"You'll be coming down the station
with me, Harry," said PC Truncheon.
"It's off to jail for you."

"Will he be out in time to compete in
the Posh Olympics?" asked Molly.

But neither PC Truncheon nor
Mrs Quibble seemed to hear.

They had been distracted by the arrival
from the kitchen of a small cowboy.

"Howdy, pardners," said the cowboy. **"There's rattlesnakes in your back garden and they're eating all the moles."**

MAX AND MOLLY LEARN A NEW WORD

Max and Molly's mum made macaroni
cheese for tea, their favourite. Dad said
he'd buy both of them a reward the next
day. PC Truncheon said they could come
and look round the police station and
Mrs Quibble said they could kick their

ball into her garden another two hundred and seventeen times if they wanted.

Only **Harry the Gent** hadn't promised them anything nice, which was understandable in the circumstances.

"I'm so proud of you," said Dad. "I still can't work out exactly how you managed to catch him in the act."

Max and Molly carried on eating. They didn't know either and they thought it was safer to keep their mouths shut.

"When I think of you being so near
a **criminal**," said Mum, shuddering.
"Anything could have happened."

There was a knock at the front door.
Mum opened it. Standing there was
Peter. And Peter's mum.

"Here's another hero," said Max and Molly's mum.

"Hero?" said Peter's mum, dragging her son into the kitchen. "He's not a hero. He's an idiot."

"Now come on, Pam..." began Dad.

"Don't you *come on* me," said Peter's mum. "I've scrubbed and scrubbed and it won't come off. Just look at his face!"

Everybody looked. Peter still had the long droopy brown moustache of a cowboy. It turned out that **INDELIBLE** meant you couldn't wash it off.

"Achoo!" said Peter.

"I think it suits him," said Molly brightly.

The looks on the adults' faces suggested they didn't agree.

"Right, you two," said Mum. "You've got some explaining to do."

Max and Molly looked at each other and sighed. Things were already getting back to normal...

The end

Turn over for
Max and Molly's Guide to making
BLACK WIDOW CRUNCHIES!

How to Make Black Widow Crunchies

(FOR YOU, YOUR FRIENDS OR MRS QUIBBLE)

You will need:
- 200g **chocolate**, broken into pieces
- 1 tablespoon **BUTTER**
- 1 teaspoon golden syrup
- 90g cornflakes or **rice crispies**
- 12 **PAPER CAKE CASES**

Before you start, ask an adult to help you. If they say no, explain just how much mess there will be if they don't. Use words like **disaster, catastrophe** and **emergency plumber**. Words like these make adults change their minds.

1. Place the **chocolate** pieces, **BUTTER** and golden syrup in a large heatproof bowl. Melt everything together, either in the microwave or by placing the bowl on top of a saucepan of simmering water.

2. Add the cornflakes or **rice crispies**, one handful at a time, stirring until they are all coated.

3. Put a heaped tablespoon of mixture into each **PAPER CASE** and put them in the fridge until set.

4. Eat, yum yum.

HOW TO MAKE BLACK WIDOW CRUNCHIES

(FOR YOUR ENEMIES OR HARRY THE GENT)

- 2 pieces toast and jam, broken into pieces
- 1 tablespoon **marmalade**
- 2 tablespoons **peanut butter**
- 90g cornflakes
- Squeeze of **grapefruit**
- 1 teaspoon sugar
- 1 teaspoon **pickle**
- 12 **PAPER CAKE CASES**
- Some plastic spiders to decorate

1. Mix it all together! Put a heaped tablespoon of mixture into each **PAPER CASE**.

2. Decorate with a spider or two.

3. Decide who deserves an extra special treat...

4. RUN!

HANNAH SHAW is precisely five foot five inches tall and was born some time in the 1980s. She is the brilliant author and illustrator of a number of picture books, as well an illustrator for young fiction. When she isn't drawing, writing or eating (far too many) chocolate biscuits, Hannah enjoys dog agility, dancing and making robot costumes.

DOMINIC BARKER is not sure how tall he is any more as his doctor tells him he is shrinking. He has a recurring nightmare in which he is attacked by extremely agile dogs dressed as robots doing the conga. They hit him with chocolate biscuits. Dominic has a good idea who to blame for this...